'Then she began to run, and she ran over the sharp stones and through the thorns, and the wild animals bounded past her . . .'

JACOB LUDWIG KARL GRIMM
Born 1785 in Hanau, Hesse-Kassel
Died 1863 in Berlin, Germany

WILLIAM KARL GRIMM
Born 1786 in Hanau, Hesse-Kassel
Died 1859 in Berlin, Germany

Taken from David Luke's translation of *Selected Tales*, first
published in 1982.

BROTHERS GRIMM IN PENGUIN CLASSICS
Selected Tales

BROTHERS GRIMM

The Robber Bridegroom

Translated by
David Luke

PENGUIN BOOKS

PENGUIN CLASSICS

Published by the Penguin Group
Penguin Books Ltd, 80 Strand, London WC2R ORL, England
Penguin Group (USA) Inc., 375 Hudson Street, New York, New York 10014, USA
Penguin Group (Canada), 90 Eglinton Avenue East, Suite 700, Toronto, Ontario,
Canada M4P 2Y3 (a division of Pearson Penguin Canada Inc.)
Penguin Ireland, 25 St Stephen's Green, Dublin 2, Ireland
(a division of Penguin Books Ltd)
Penguin Group (Australia), 707 Collins Street, Melbourne, Victoria 3008, Australia
(a division of Pearson Australia Group Pty Ltd)
Penguin Books India Pvt Ltd, 11 Community Centre, Panchsheel Park,
New Delhi – 110 017, India
Penguin Group (NZ), 67 Apollo Drive, Rosedale, Auckland 0632, New Zealand
(a division of Pearson New Zealand Ltd)
Penguin Books (South Africa) (Pty) Ltd, Block D, Rosebank Office Park,
181 Jan Smuts Avenue, Parktown North, Gauteng 2193, South Africa

Penguin Books Ltd, Registered Offices: 80 Strand, London WC2R ORL, England

www.penguin.com

This selection published in Penguin Classics 2015
002

Translation copyright © 1982 by David Luke

The moral right of the translator has been asserted

Set in 9.5/13 pt Baskerville 10 Pro
Typeset by Jouve (UK), Milton Keynes
Printed in Great Britain by Clays Ltd, St Ives plc

A CIP catalogue record for this book is available from the British Library

ISBN: 978-0-141-39857-0

www.greenpenguin.co.uk

Contents

The Master Huntsman

Once upon a time there was a young fellow who had learnt the locksmith's trade, and he told his father that he would like to go out into the world now and try his luck. 'Yes,' said his father, 'that suits me,' and he gave him some money to take with him. So he travelled around looking for work. After a time he began to find that the locksmith's trade was not to his liking and no longer suited him, but he fancied the idea of hunting. On his wanderings he met a huntsman in a green coat, who asked him where he had come from and where he was going. The lad replied that he was a journeyman locksmith, but that he no longer cared for the trade and would like to learn hunting instead; would the huntsman take him on as an apprentice? 'Oh yes, if you'll come along with me.' So the young lad went with him, signed on with him for several years and learnt hunting. After that he wanted to go out and try his luck again, and the huntsman gave him an air-gun instead of wages, but it was a special kind of gun: if he shot with it he would never miss. So he set off and presently came to a very large forest. There was no reaching the end of it in one day, so when evening fell he perched on a tall tree to be out of reach of the wild beasts. At about midnight he thought he saw a faint light gleaming some way off; he peered at it through the branches and noted carefully where it was; then he took off his hat and threw it down in the direction of the light, to mark which way he should walk when he got down from the tree. Then he climbed down, walked towards his hat, put it on again and continued in the same direction. The further he walked the bigger the light grew, and when he got near it he saw that it was an enormous fire, and round it sat three giants who had spitted an ox and were roasting it. And one of them said: 'Let me just taste whether the meat's done yet.' And he tore off a piece and was about to put it in his mouth when the huntsman shot it out of his hand. 'Well, look at that,' said the giant, 'the wind blew the meat right out of my hand.' And he pulled off another piece, but just as he was going to take a bite the huntsman shot it away too. At this the giant slapped his neighbour's face and exclaimed angrily: 'Will you stop snatching my food!' 'I didn't snatch it,' said the other, 'I think it was shot down by a sniper.' The giant took a third piece, but the moment he had it in his hand the huntsman shot it down too. The giants said to each other: 'That must be a good marksman if he can shoot the meat right out of our mouths; he'd be useful to us.' And they shouted: 'Come on over here, sharpshooter, sit down at the fire with us and eat your fill, we won't touch you; but if you don't come and we fetch you by force, that'll be the end of you.' So the lad came over to them and told them he was a trained huntsman, and that whatever he took aim at with his gun he would hit it without fail. Then they said that if he would go along with them he would be well looked after. They told him that on the far side of the forest there was a wide river, and beyond it stood a tower, and in the tower lived a beautiful princess whom they intended to carry off. 'All right,' he said, 'I'll soon get hold of her for you.' 'But there's a snag in it,' they added. 'There's a little dog there, and it starts barking as soon as anyone comes near the place, and as soon as it barks everyone at the king's court wakes up, and that's why we can't get in. Will you undertake to shoot the dog?' 'Yes,' he answered, 'that's child's play to me.' Then he took a boat and crossed the water, and when he was about to land the little dog came running towards him and was just going to bark when he seized his gun and shot it dead. When the giants saw this they were delighted, thinking the princess was as good as theirs; but the huntsman first wanted to see how things stood, and told them to wait outside till he called them. Then he went into the castle; there was not a sound to be heard and everyone was asleep. In the first room he entered there was a sword hanging on the wall: it was made of pure silver, and on it was a golden star and the king's name, and beside it on a table lay a sealed letter. He opened the letter, which said that whoever had the sword would be able to kill any enemy he met. So he took the sword from the wall, buckled it on and went further till he came to the room where the princess was lying asleep: and she was so beautiful that he stopped and gazed at her and held his breath. He said to himself: 'It would be wrong to let those savage giants get an innocent maiden into their power: they have wicked intentions.' He looked round again and saw a pair of slippers under her bed: on the right slipper was her father's name and a star and on the left her own name and a star. And she was wearing a long silk kerchief embroidered in gold, with her father's name on the right side and on the left her own name, all embroidered in golden letters. Then the huntsman took a pair of scissors and cut off the right-hand end of the kerchief and put it in his knapsack, into which he also put her right slipper with the king's name on it. Now the maiden was still lying there asleep, and she was all sewn into her nightgown: so he cut off a small piece of her nightgown and put it with the other things, but all this he did without touching her. Then he left her to sleep on in peace, and when he got back to the gate the giants were still out there waiting for him, thinking he would bring the princess to them. But he called out to them to come in, saying that the princess was already in his power, and that he couldn't open the door for them but that there was a hole they must crawl through. So when the first of them came to the hole the huntsman wound the giant's hair round his hand, pulled his head through, drew his sword and cut it off with one blow; then he pulled the whole body in. After this he called to the second giant and cut his head off too, and finally he did the same to the third. Feeling glad to have saved the beautiful princess from her enemies, he cut out the giants' tongues and put them in his knapsack. After that he thought: I'll go home to my father and show him what I've done already, then I'll travel about in the world; if God has good fortune in store for me, it'll come to me sooner or later.

But in the castle the king woke up and saw the three giants lying there dead. He went to his daughter's bed-chamber, woke her up and asked her who it could have been that had killed the giants. She said: 'Father dear, I don't know, I was asleep.' Then when she got up and was going to put on her slippers she found the right slipper missing, and when she looked at her kerchief she found that the right-hand end of it was missing, and when she looked at her nightgown a piece had been cut out of that too. The king ordered the whole court to be assembled, including his soldiers and everyone who was there, and asked who had saved his daughter and killed the giants. Now in his army he had a captain, an ugly one-eyed fellow, and he claimed to have done it. Then the old king said that if he had done such a deed he must also marry his daughter. But the princess said: 'Dear father, rather than marry that man I will go as far away into the world as my legs will carry me.' The king said that if she refused to marry him she must take off her royal garments and put on peasant's clothes and leave the court; and he ordered her to go to a potter and set herself up selling earthenware pots and plates. So she took off her royal garments and went to a potter and borrowed a lot of earthenware crockery from him, promising that if she had sold it by evening she would pay him for it. The king also ordered her to sit down at a street corner and offer it for sale there, and then he arranged with some carters to drive right through the middle of it and break it into a thousand pieces. So when the princess had put out her wares on the street, the carts came and smashed them to smithereens. She began to cry and said: 'Oh God help me, how shall I pay the potter now!' The king had done this in order to force her to marry the captain; but instead she went back to the potter and asked if he would lend her some more things. He refused to do so until she had paid for the first lot. So she went to her father and wept and lamented and said she would go away into the world. So he said: 'I'll have a hut built for you out there in the forest, and you shall live in it for the rest of your life and cook meals for everyone, but you are to accept no payment for them.' When the hut was ready a sign was hung out over the door, and on it was written: 'Free meals today, tomorrow you pay.' She lived in the hut for a long time, and word went round in the world that here was a young lady who cooked free meals and that this was written up over the door. The huntsman heard this story too and thought: This is a chance for me; after all, I'm poor and I've no money. So he took his air-gun and his knapsack, which still had in it all the things he had once taken away from the castle as proofs, and went into the forest; and sure enough he found the hut with the sign: 'Free meals today, tomorrow you pay.' Wearing the sword with which he had cut off the heads of the three giants, he went in and asked for something to eat. He was delighted to see the beautiful girl; and beautiful she certainly was. She asked where he came from and where he was going and he told her that he was travelling about in the world. Then she asked him where he had got the sword, because it had her father's name on it. He asked if she was the king's daughter. 'Yes,' she answered. 'With this sword,' he said, 'I cut off the heads of three giants.' And as proof he fetched their tongues out of his knapsack, then he showed her the slipper and the pieces he had cut from her kerchief and her nightgown. At this she was overjoyed and said he was the man who had saved her. So they went together to the castle and asked to speak to the old king, and she took him to her bedchamber and told him that it was the huntsman who had really rescued her from the giants. And when the old king saw all the proofs he could no longer doubt it, and said that he was glad to have found out what had happened, and that he would now give his daughter in marriage to the huntsman. The princess consented to this very gladly. Then they gave him fine clothes as if he were a visiting lord, and the king ordered a banquet. At table the captain sat down on the princess's left and the huntsman on her right, and the captain supposed that he was a gentleman from abroad who was visiting them. When they had eaten and drunk, the old king told the captain that he would like to set him a riddle to guess. 'If a man,' said the king, 'were to claim to have killed three giants, and were to be asked where the giants' tongues were, and were to be shown their heads and see that the tongues were missing, what would be the reason for that?' The captain replied: 'I suppose the giants had no tongues.' 'Not so,' said the king, 'every creature has a tongue.' And then he asked the captain what fate such a man would deserve. The captain answered: 'He would deserve to be torn to pieces.' Then the king said: 'You have passed sentence on yourself.' So the captain was arrested and torn apart by four horses; and the princess was married to the huntsman. After the wedding he went and fetched his mother and father, and they lived happily with their son, and after the old king's death he inherited the kingdom.

The Robber Bridegroom

Once upon a time there was a miller who had a beautiful daughter, and when she grew up he was anxious to see her well married and provided for. He thought: If a proper suitor comes along and asks for her hand, he shall have her. Before long a suitor turned up who seemed to be very rich, and since the miller could find nothing against him he promised him his daughter. But the girl didn't really take to him as a girl should to her betrothed bridegroom: she didn't trust him, and her heart contracted with horror every time she looked at him or thought of him. One day he said to her: 'You're my betrothed bride and yet you never even come to visit me.' The girl replied: 'I don't know, sir, where your house is.' And the bridegroom said: 'My house is out there in the dark forest.' She tried to think of excuses and said she wouldn't be able to find the way there. The bridegroom said: 'Next Sunday you must come out to visit me. I've invited the guests already, and to help you find your way through the forest I'll put down a trail of ashes for you.' When Sunday came and she had to set out, she felt afraid without really knowing why, and filled both her pockets with peas and lentils to mark the path. When she came to the edge of the forest, she found that ashes had been scattered and she followed the trail, but at every step, left and right, she threw a few peas on the ground. She walked nearly all day till she came to the middle of the forest, where it was darkest of all, and here she found an isolated house. She didn't like the look of it, it seemed gloomy and sinister. She went in, but there was no one there and everything was very silent. Suddenly a voice called out:

> 'Go home, go home, my lady bride,
> This is a house where murderers hide.'

Looking up, she saw that the voice was that of a bird hanging in a cage on the wall. It called out again:

> 'Go home, go home, my lady bride,
> This is a house where murderers hide.'

Then the fair bride walked on from room to room and explored the whole house, but it was all empty and not a soul was to be seen. Finally she reached the cellar, and there a very old woman was sitting wagging her head. 'Can you not tell me, good woman,' asked the girl, 'whether my bridegroom lives here?' 'Oh, you poor child,' answered the old woman, 'what a place you have strayed to! This is a den of murderers. You think you're a bride soon to be wedded, but it's death you're going to wed. Look, I've had to fill that great cauldron with water and put it on the fire; once they have you in their power, they'll chop you up without mercy and cook you and eat you, for they're eaters of human flesh. If I don't take pity on you and save you, you're lost.'

So saying, the old woman hid the girl behind a huge barrel where she couldn't be seen. 'Be as quiet as a mouse,' she said, 'don't move and don't stir, or it'll be the end of you. In the night, when the robbers are asleep, we'll escape; I've waited long enough for a chance myself.' Scarcely had she said this when the godless crew returned home. They were dragging another young maiden with them; they were drunk, and paid no heed to her screams and lamentations. They gave her some wine to drink, three glasses full, one of white and one of red and one of yellow, and that made her heart burst. Then they tore off her pretty clothes, laid her out on a table, hacked her fair body to pieces and sprinkled them with salt. The poor bride hidden behind the barrel trembled and shuddered, for she saw clearly what a fate the robbers had had in store for her. One of them noticed a gold ring on the murdered girl's little finger, and as it didn't come off at once when he pulled, he took an axe and chopped the finger off. But the finger jumped up into the air and jumped right over the barrel and fell straight into the bride's lap. The robber took a candle and began looking for it, but he couldn't find it. Then another of them said: 'Did you look behind the big barrel as well?' But the old woman exclaimed: 'Come along and eat, and leave searching till tomorrow; the finger won't run away.'

The robbers said: 'The old woman's right,' and stopped looking for it and sat down to their supper; and the old woman poured a sleeping draught into their wine, so that they were soon lying down in the cellar asleep and snoring. When the bride heard this, she came out from behind the barrel. She had to step over the sleeping men, who were lying on the ground in rows, and she was terrified that she might wake one up. But God helped her and she got past them safely. The old woman came upstairs with her and opened the door, and they hurried away from that murderers' den as fast as they could. The wind had blown away the ash trail, but the peas and lentils had sprouted up and showed them the way in the moonlight. They walked all night and reached the mill in the morning, and the girl told her father everything that had happened.

When the day came on which the wedding was to take place the bridegroom appeared, and the miller had had all his friends and relatives invited. As they sat at dinner, everyone in turn was asked to tell a story. The bride sat silent and didn't speak a word. Then the bridegroom said to her: 'Well, my love, can you think of nothing? Why don't you tell us a story too?' She answered: 'I will tell you a dream I had. I was walking alone through a forest and finally came to a house with not a living soul in it, but on a wall there was a bird in a cage that called out:

"Go home, go home, my lady bride,
This is a house where murderers hide."

It said these words to me twice. My dear, it was only a dream. Then I explored all the rooms, and they were all empty and it was all so uncanny; finally I went down to the cellar and found a very old woman sitting there wagging her head. I asked her: "Does my bridegroom live in this house?" She answered: "Oh, you poor child, you have come to a den of murderers; your bridegroom lives here, but he intends to chop you up and kill you and then cook you and eat you." My dear, it was only a dream. But the old woman hid me behind a big barrel, and no sooner was I hidden there than the robbers came home dragging a girl with them. They gave her three kinds of wine to drink, white and red and yellow, and that made her heart burst. My dear, it was only a dream. Then they pulled off her pretty clothes, chopped her fair body in pieces on a table and sprinkled them with salt. My dear, it was only a dream. And one of the robbers saw that on her ring-finger there was still a gold ring, and because it was hard to get off he took an axe and chopped it off; but the finger jumped up into the air and jumped right over the big barrel and fell into my lap. And here is the finger with the ring on it.' So saying, she took it out and showed it to the company.

The robber, who had turned white as a sheet as she told her story, jumped up and tried to escape, but the guests seized him and handed him over to the authorities. Then he and his whole band were brought to justice for their foul deeds.

The Devil's Three Golden Hairs

Once upon a time there was a poor woman who gave birth to a little son, and because he came into the world with a caul it was prophesied that in his fourteenth year he would marry the king's daughter. Soon after this it happened that the king came to that village and no one knew it was the king, and when he asked the people what had been happening recently, they answered: 'There was a child born the other day with a caul, and that'll bring him luck in everything he does. It's even been prophesied that in his fourteenth year he'll marry the king's daughter.' The king, who had a wicked heart and was angered by this prophecy, went to the parents, pretended to be very friendly and said: 'You poor folk, let me have your child, I'll look after him well.' At first they refused, but the stranger offered to pay a lot of money for the boy, and they thought: He's a fortune-child, so it's bound to turn out all right for him anyway. So in the end they consented and handed him over.

The king put the child in a box and rode off with him till he came to a deep river; and here he threw the box into the water, thinking: Well, I've rid my daughter of that unexpected suitor. But the box didn't sink, it floated like a little boat, and not a drop of water got into it. It drifted downstream as far as a mill within two leagues of the king's capital, and here it got caught against the dam. Luckily a miller's boy was standing there and noticed it, and he pulled it ashore with a hook, thinking he had found a treasure chest; but when he opened it, there lay a fine little boy looking as fresh as a daisy. He took him to the miller and his wife, and as they had no children of their own they were delighted and said: 'He's a gift from God.' They took good care of the foundling, and he grew up as good as gold.

It so happened that one day the king came into the mill to shelter from a storm, and he asked the miller and his wife whether the big sturdy boy was their son. 'No,' they answered, 'he's a foundling. Fourteen years ago he came floating down to the mill dam in a box, and our servant pulled him out of the water.' Then the king realized this was the very same fortune-child he had thrown into the river, and he said: 'Good people, could the lad not take a letter for me to the queen? I'll pay him two gold pieces.' 'As my lord the king commands,' they replied, and told the boy to be ready to leave. Then the king wrote a letter to the queen which said: 'As soon as the boy carrying this letter arrives, he is to be killed and buried, and all that is to be over and done with before I get back.'

The boy set out with this letter, but lost his way and in

the evening found himself in a great forest. In the dark-
ness he saw a faint light, made his way towards it and
came to a small house. When he entered, an old woman
was sitting by the fire all by herself. She was startled to
see the lad and said: 'Where are you from and where are
you going?' 'I'm from the mill,' he answered, 'and I'm
on my way to the queen with a letter I have to take to
her; but I've lost my way in the forest, so I'd like to stay
the night here.' 'You poor boy,' said the woman, 'this
house belongs to a gang of robbers, and when they get
home they'll kill you.' 'I don't mind who comes,' said the
boy, 'I'm not afraid; but I'm so tired that I can't go any
further.' And he lay down on a bench and went to sleep.
Presently the robbers came in and asked angrily what
strange boy this was lying there. The old woman said:
'Oh, he's just an innocent child, he's got lost in the wood,
so I felt sorry for him and let him stay. He's been told to
take a letter to the queen.' The robbers opened the letter
and read it, and found that it said that as soon as the boy
arrived he was to be put to death. At this the hard-hearted
robbers took pity on him, and their leader tore up the
letter and wrote another which said that as soon as the
boy arrived he was to be married to the king's daughter.
Then they let him lie there in peace till the next morning,
and when he woke up they gave him the letter and showed
him the right way. But when the queen had received the
letter and read it, she did what it told her to do: she
ordered a magnificent wedding feast and the princess was

married to the fortune-child. And since he was a handsome and good-natured young man, she was quite happy
and content to live with him.

After a time the king came back to his palace and saw
that the prophecy had been fulfilled and that the
fortune-child was married to his daughter. 'How did this
come about?' he demanded. 'I gave quite different orders
in my letter.' So the queen handed him the letter and
invited him to see for himself what was in it. The king
read the letter and saw at once that it had been exchanged
for the other one. He asked the young man what had
happened to the letter he had been given, and why he
had brought a different one instead. 'I know nothing
about it,' the boy answered. 'It must have been exchanged
during the night, when I was sleeping in the forest.' The
king said in a rage: 'You shan't get away with it as easily
as that. Anyone who wants my daughter for his wife has
got to go down into Hell and fetch me three golden hairs
from the Devil's head. That's what I want, and if you bring
them to me you shall keep my daughter.' The king hoped
in this way to be rid of him for ever. But the fortune-child
answered: 'I'll fetch the golden hairs, I'm not afraid of
the Devil.' With that he took his leave and began his
journey.

His road took him to a great city, where the watchman at the gate questioned him about his trade and about
what he knew. 'I know everything,' replied the fortune-
child. 'In that case you can do us a favour,' said the

watchman. 'You can tell us why the fountain in our market place that used to have wine running out of it has dried up, so that we don't even get water from it now.' 'I'll tell you that,' he answered, 'but you must wait till I return.' Then he went on and came to another city, and again the watchman at the gate asked him what his trade was and what he knew. 'I know everything,' he answered. 'Then you can do us a favour and tell us why a tree in our city that used to bear golden apples doesn't even grow leaves any more.' 'I'll tell you that,' he answered, 'but you must wait till I return.' Then he went on and came to a wide river that he had to cross. The ferryman asked him what his trade was and what he knew. 'I know everything,' he answered. 'Then you can do me a favour,' said the ferryman, 'and tell me why I have to keep on pushing this boat to and fro and no one ever takes over the job from me.' 'I'll tell you that,' he answered, 'but you must wait till I return.'

When he had crossed the river he found the entrance to Hell. Everything inside was black and sooty, and the Devil wasn't at home, but there sat his grandmother in a big armchair. 'What do you want?' she asked him, and she didn't look all that fierce. 'I'd like three golden hairs, please, from the Devil's head,' he answered, 'otherwise I won't be allowed to keep my wife.' 'That's a bold request,' said she. 'If the Devil comes home and finds you here, you'll be for it; but I'm sorry for you, so I'll see if I can help you.' She changed him into an ant and said: 'Crawl into the fold of my skirt, you'll be safe there.' 'Yes,' he answered, 'that's all right, but there are three things I'd like to know as well: why has a fountain that used to flow with wine dried up, so that it doesn't even give water now? And why has a tree that used to bear golden apples even stopped growing leaves? And why is it that a ferryman has to keep on crossing the river and no one ever takes over the job from him?' 'Those are hard questions,' she answered, 'but just keep quiet and stay still and pay attention to what the Devil says when I pull his three golden hairs out.'

When evening fell the Devil came home, and he'd no sooner entered than he noticed that things were not as usual. 'I smell human flesh, I smell it,' he said. 'There's something going on here.' Then he searched in every corner but couldn't find anything. His grandmother scolded him. 'I've only just done the sweeping,' she said, 'and tidied the whole place, and now you're messing it all up again. You're forever smelling human flesh! Sit down and eat your supper.' When he had eaten and drunk, he felt tired and lay down with his head in his grandmother's lap and told her to pick some of the lice out of his hair. It wasn't long before he fell asleep and started puffing and snoring. Then the old woman seized a golden hair, tweaked it out and laid it down beside her. 'Ow!' shrieked the Devil, 'what do you think you're doing?' 'I had a bad dream,' his grandmother answered, 'so I grabbed at your hair.' 'Well, what were you dreaming about?' asked the

Devil. 'I dreamt there was a fountain in a market place, and wine used to come from it, but now it's dried up and won't even give them water; what can be the reason for that?' 'Ho, ho, if only they knew!' answered the Devil. 'There's a toad sitting under a stone in the well; if they kill it the wine will flow again all right.' His grandmother picked out some more of his lice till he fell asleep and started snoring fit to shake the windows. Then she tweaked out the second golden hair. 'Ow-wow! What are you doing?' shrieked the Devil in a rage. 'Never mind, never mind,' she said. 'I did it in my sleep, I was dreaming.' 'What were you dreaming about this time?' he asked. 'I dreamt about a kingdom where there was a fruit-tree that used to bear golden apples, and now it won't even grow leaves. I wonder what can have caused that?' 'Ho ho, if only they knew!' answered the Devil. 'There's a mouse gnawing at its root; if they kill the mouse the golden apples will soon grow again, but if it goes on gnawing the whole tree will wither. And now leave me in a peace, you and your dreams; if you wake me up again I'll box your ears.' His grandmother spoke to him soothingly and picked out some more lice till he was asleep and snoring. Then she seized the third golden hair and tweaked it out. The Devil jumped up with a yell and began to set about her, but she calmed him down again and said: 'How can one help having bad dreams!' 'What have you been dreaming now?' he asked, his curiosity getting the better of him. 'I dreamt there was a ferryman complaining that he has to keep on crossing the river and no one takes over the job from him. What can be the cause of that?' 'Ho ho, the stupid lout!' answered the Devil. 'When someone comes and wants to cross, he must just put the oar into his hand, and then the other man will have to do the ferrying and he'll be free.' So now that his grandmother had plucked out the three golden hairs and the three questions had been answered, she left the old dragon in peace, and he slept till daybreak.

When the Devil had gone out again, the old woman took the ant from the fold in her skirt and gave the fortune-child his human form back. 'Here are the three golden hairs,' she said, 'and I expect you heard what the Devil said about your three questions.' 'Yes,' he answered, 'I heard it all and I'll remember it well.' 'So that's your problem solved,' she said, 'and now you can be off.' He thanked the old woman for her much needed help and climbed up out of Hell, feeling very pleased with his success. When he came to the ferryman, he was asked for his promised answer. 'First take me across,' said the fortune-child, 'and then I'll tell you how you can be released.' And when he had got to the opposite bank, he gave him the Devil's advice: 'Next time someone comes to be ferried across, just put the oar into his hand.' He went on and came to the city where the barren tree was, and there too the watchman demanded his answer. So he told him what he had heard from the Devil: 'Kill the mouse that's gnawing at its root, and it'll bear golden apples again.' The watchman thanked him, and as a reward gave him two donkeys laden with gold and told them to follow him. Finally he came to the city where the fountain had dried up. So he told the watchman as the Devil had said: 'There's a toad sitting in it under a stone; you must look for it and kill it, and then you'll get plenty of wine from the fountain again.' The watchman thanked him, and he gave him two donkeys laden with gold as well.

Then at last the fortune-child got home to his wife, who was delighted to see him again and to hear how well everything had gone. He took the king what he had asked for, the Devil's three golden hairs, and when the king saw the four donkey-loads of gold he was very pleased indeed and said: 'Now that you have fulfilled all the conditions you can keep my daughter. But, my dear son-in-law, won't you tell me how you came by all that gold? You have brought back very great treasure!' 'I crossed a river,' he answered, 'and that's where I got it from; it's lying all along the bank instead of sand.' 'Could I fetch some for myself as well?' asked the king with great eagerness. 'As much as you want, sir,' replied the young man. 'There's a ferryman on the river, get him to ferry you over and you'll be able to fill your sacks at the other side.' The king, his heart filled with greed, set off in great haste, and when he came to the river he beckoned to the ferryman to take him across. The ferryman came and told him to get into the boat, and when they reached the opposite bank he handed him the oar and jumped out. And after that the king had to go on ferrying as a punishment for his sins.

'Is he still doing it?' 'Why not? I don't suppose anyone has taken the oar from him.'

The Six Servants

Long ago there lived an old queen who was a sorceress and her daughter was the most beautiful maiden under the sun. But the old queen's one idea was to lure people to their destruction, and when a suitor came she would say that any man wanting to marry her daughter must first perform a task, or his life would be forfeit. Many were dazzled by the maiden's beauty and did try their luck, but they failed to perform the task the queen set them, and then they were shown no mercy: they had to kneel at the block and have their heads cut off. Now there was a prince who had also heard of the maiden's beauty, and he said to his father: 'Let me go and try to win her hand.' 'No, no!' said the king, 'if you go, you will be going to your death.' Then his son took to his bed and became mortally ill and lay there for seven years, and no doctor could help him. When his father saw that there was no more hope, he said to him very sorrowfully: 'Go and try your fortune, for I know no other way to help you.' When his son heard that, he rose from his bed fully restored to health, and joyfully set out on his journey.

It happened that as he was riding over open country he saw something on the ground some way off that looked like a huge haystack, and when he got nearer he could see that it was the belly of a man lying on his back, a paunch the size of a small mountain. When the Fat Man saw the traveller he sat up and said: 'If you need someone, sir, then take me into your service.' The prince answered: 'What use can I make of a great unwieldy fellow like you?' 'Oh,' said the Fat Man, 'that's a mere trifle: when I feel really expansive, I'm three thousand times this size.' 'If that's so,' said the prince, 'then I can use you, come along with me.' So the Fat Man came along with the prince, and after a while they found another man lying on the ground with one ear pressed against the grass. 'What are you doing there?' asked the prince. 'I'm listening,' answered the man. 'What are you listening for so attentively?' 'I'm listening to what's going on in the world at this moment, for nothing escapes my ears, I can even hear the grass growing.' The prince asked: 'Tell me, what do you hear at the court of the old queen who has the beautiful daughter?' The man answered: 'I can hear the whistling of a sword through the air as it strikes off a suitor's head.' The prince said: 'I can use you, come along with me.' So they travelled on, and presently they saw a pair of feet lying on the ground, and part of the legs as well, but they couldn't see the other end of whoever they belonged to. When they had gone on quite some distance they came to the body, and finally to the head. 'Well!' said the prince. 'What a tall whopper you are!' 'Oh,' said the Tall Man, 'this is nothing: when I really stretch my limbs I'm three thousand times this height, taller than the highest mountain on earth. I'll be glad to serve you, sir, if you'll take me on.' 'Come with us,' said the prince, 'I can use you.' They travelled on and found a man sitting at the roadside with his eyes blindfolded. The prince asked him: 'Have you got such weak eyes that you can't look at the daylight?' 'No,' answered the man, 'I can't take off the blindfold because my eyes are so powerful that when they look at anything it explodes. If that's any use to you, sir, I'll gladly serve you.' 'Come with us,' answered the prince, 'I can use you.' They travelled on and found a man lying in the full heat of the sun shivering with cold and shaking in every limb. 'How can you be shivering in this hot sunshine?' asked the prince. 'Oh dear me,' replied the man, 'I have a quite different constitution: the hotter it is, the colder I get and my bones freeze to the very marrow, but the colder it is the hotter I get. If there's ice all round me I can't bear the heat, and if it's fire I can't stand the cold.' 'You're a strange fellow,' said the prince, 'but if you'd like to serve me, come along with us.' They travelled on and saw a man standing and craning his neck, gazing in all directions and away into the distance. The prince asked: 'What are you so busy looking for?' The man replied: 'I've got such sharp eyes that I can see right beyond all the forests and fields and valleys and mountains and right through the whole world.' The prince said: 'If you'd like to, then come along with me, because you're just what I still needed.'

The prince with his six servants now entered the city where the old queen lived. He didn't tell her who he was, but said: 'Madam, if you will give me your beautiful daughter, I will perform whatever you command me.' The sorceress was glad to have such a handsome youth falling into her snares again, and she said: 'I will set you three tasks, and if you succeed in each of them you shall become my daughter's lord and husband.' 'What is the first task to be?' he asked. 'I want you to fetch me back a ring I dropped into the Red Sea.' So the prince went home to his servants and said: 'The first task's not easy, I'm to fetch a ring out of the Red Sea; now tell me how to do that.' The Sharpsighted Man said: 'I'll find out where it is,' and after looking down into the sea he told them: 'There it is, caught on a jagged piece of rock.' The Tall Man carried them to the shore of the Red Sea and said: 'I could fetch it out all right if I could only see it.' 'Well, if that's the only problem!' exclaimed the Fat Man, and he lay down and put his mouth to the water. The waves poured into it as if into a bottomless pit, and he drank up the whole sea till it was as dry as a field. The Tall Man stooped down slightly and picked up the ring. The prince was delighted once he had it, and he took it to the old queen, who was astonished and said: 'Yes, that's the right ring. You've been successful with your first task, but now here is the second. You see there on the field in front of my castle, there are three hundred fat oxen grazing, and these you must devour, skin and bone and hair and horns and all; and down in my cellar there are three hundred casks of wine, which you must drink with the meat; and if you leave so much as one single ox-hair or one little drop of the wine, your life will be forfeit.' The prince said: 'And may I invite no guests? No meal is tasty without company.' The old woman laughed maliciously and replied: 'You may invite one guest to keep you company, but not more than one.'

So the prince went to his servants and said to the Fat Man: 'Today you are to be my guest and eat your fill for once.' So the Fat Man expanded and ate up the three hundred oxen, leaving not so much as a hair, then asked if breakfast was all he was to get. The wine he drank straight from the barrels without needing a glass, and finished it right to the last drop. When the meal was over, the prince went to the old queen and told her that he had performed the second task. She was amazed and said: 'You have done better than any of the others; but there's still one task left.' And she thought: You'll not escape me, you'll not keep your head on your shoulders. 'Tonight,' she said, 'I shall bring my daughter to you in your room, and you shall put your arm round her; but as you sit there with her beware of falling asleep, for I shall come at exactly twelve o'clock, and if she's no longer in your arms then, you will have lost.' The prince thought: This task is easy, I'm sure I'll be able to keep my eyes open; but he called his servants and told them what the old queen had said, adding: 'Who knows what tricks she may be up to? We had better be cautious, and you must keep watch and see to it that once the maiden is in my room she doesn't get out of it again.' When night fell the old woman came with her daughter and left her in the prince's arms; then the Tall Man made a ring of himself and lay down round both of them, and the Fat Man stood in front of the door so that no living soul could get in. So there they both sat, and the maiden didn't speak a word, but the moon shone through the window on to her face so that he could see her wonderful beauty. He did nothing but gaze at her, full of joy and love, and his eyes never once felt weary. That lasted till eleven o'clock; and then the old queen cast a spell on all of them that made them fall asleep, and at the same moment the maiden vanished.

They remained fast asleep till a quarter to twelve, and then the spell lost its power and they all woke up again. 'Alack and alas!' cried the prince, 'now I am lost!' And his faithful servants began to lament as well, but the Listener said: 'Be quiet, let me listen.' And he listened for a moment, then said: 'She's sitting inside a rock three hundred hours journey from here, bewailing her fate. Only you can help her, Tall Man; if you stretch yourself you'll be there in a couple of steps.' 'Yes,' answered the Tall Man, 'but our friend with the powerful eyes must come along as well, so that we can get rid of the rock.' So the

Tall Man hoisted the Blindfolded Man on to his back, and in an instant, before you could snap your fingers, they had arrived in front of the enchanted rock. At once the Tall Man unbound the eyes of his companion, who merely had to look about him and the rock exploded into smithereens. The Tall Man picked up the princess and carried her back to the palace in no time, then he fetched his companion with equal speed, and before the clock struck twelve they were all sitting there as before, wide awake and in high spirits. When twelve struck, the old sorceress came creeping in with a mocking expression on her face, as if to say: 'Now I've got him.' For she thought her daughter was sitting inside the rock three hundred hours away. But when she saw her daughter in the prince's arms, she was dumbfounded and exclaimed: 'This is a man with more power than I have.' But there was nothing she could say, and she had to consent to let him marry the maiden. But she whispered into her daughter's ear: 'What a disgrace for you to have to obey a common man, and not to be able to take a husband of your own choice.'

At this the maiden's proud heart was filled with anger and she began to plan revenge. Next morning she had three hundred cords of wood piled up, and said to the prince: 'You have performed the three tasks, but I'll not become your wife until one of you is willing to sit in the middle of a fire made of that pile of wood.' She thought: None of his servants will burn himself to death, and for love of me he will sit in it himself, and then I shall be free. But the servants said: 'We've all done something now except the Freezer, so it's his turn to help.' And they seated him in the middle of the pile of faggots and set it alight. The fire began to burn, and it burnt for three days till it had burnt up all the wood; and when the flames died down, there was the Freezer standing among the ashes trembling like an aspen leaf and saying: 'I've never endured such cold in all my life, I'd have frozen to death if it had gone on longer.'

After this no further excuse could be found, and the beautiful maiden had to accept the unknown young man as her husband. But as they were driving to the church the old queen said: 'I'll not bear the disgrace of it,' and she sent troops after the bride with orders to shoot down all opposition and bring her daughter back to her. But the Listener had pricked up his ears and heard these secret instructions. 'What shall we do?' he asked the Fat Man. The Fat Man knew what to do: he gave one or two belches and spewed out behind the carriage some of the sea water he had drunk. The result was a huge lake in which the troops got stuck and drowned. When the sorceress heard this she sent out her armoured cavalry, but the Listener heard the clanking of their armour and uncovered the eyes of the Blindfolded Man, who gave the enemy a rather sharp look that made them disintegrate like glass. After that they drove on without further interference, and after the pair had been wedded in the church the six servants took leave of their master, saying: 'You've got what you wanted, sir, and you no longer need us: we'll travel on and try our luck.'

Half an hour's distance before the royal palace was a village, and outside it a swineherd was tending his pigs. When they arrived here, the prince said to his wife: 'Do you actually know who I am? I am not a prince but a swineherd, and that man there with the pigs is my father. The two of us will have to do our share of the work too and help him to look after them.' Then he stopped with her at an inn, and secretly told the innkeeper and his wife that during the night they were to take her royal clothes away from her. When she woke next morning she had nothing to put on, and the landlady gave her an old skirt and a pair of old woollen stockings, even acting as if this were a great favour and saying: 'If it weren't for your husband, you'd have got nothing from me at all.' Then she believed that he really was a swineherd and kept the pigs with him, and thought: I've deserved this by my pride and arrogance. That lasted a week and she couldn't bear it any longer, for her feet were all covered with sores. Then some servants came and asked if she knew who her husband was. 'Yes,' she answered, 'he's a swineherd and he's just gone out to try and sell some ribbons and laces.' But they said: 'Come with us, we'll take you to him.' And they took her up into the palace, and when she entered the hall her husband was standing there in royal clothing. But she didn't recognize him till he fell on her neck, kissed her and said: 'I suffered so much for you, so I wanted you to suffer a bit for me.' And now the wedding was really celebrated, and your storyteller wishes he'd been there too.

The Bremen Town Band

A man had a donkey who had been patiently hauling sacks of grain to the mill for many a long year, but now his strength was failing and he was becoming less and less fit for work. His master was thinking of sparing his feed and getting rid of him; but the donkey sensed that there was trouble afoot, so he ran away and set out towards Bremen, reckoning that he might get a job there in the town band. When he'd been on his way for a little while, he came across a hound lying by the roadside and panting as if he'd been running very hard. 'Well now, Buster,' asked the donkey, 'what are you puffing and blowing like that for?' 'Oh,' said the dog, 'I'm old and getting weaker day by day, and I'm no good at hunting any more, so my master was going to kill me: and so I ran away, but how shall I earn my living now?' 'I'll tell you what,' said the donkey, 'I'm on my way to Bremen to join the town band: come with me and let them sign you up in it too. I'll play the lute and you can bang the drums.' The dog accepted this invitation, and on they went. Before long they found a cat sitting by the roadside making a face like three rainy days in a row. 'Now then, Mr Whiskerwiper, what's happened to make you look so sour?' asked the donkey. 'How do you expect me to look when my life's in danger?' answered the cat. 'Just because I'm not so young as I was and my teeth aren't as sharp as they used to be and I'd sooner sit by the fire and purr than chase about after mice, my mistress tried to drown me. I managed to escape of course, but now what's to be done and where am I to go?' 'Come with us to Bremen: you sing very good serenades, so they'll take you on in the town band.' The cat thought this a good idea and joined them. Next our three refugees passed a farm, and there was the cock sitting on the gate crowing its head off. 'What a horrible noise you're making,' said the donkey, 'what's it all about?' 'I've been forecasting fine weather,' said the cock, 'because it's today Our Lady does her washing and wants to hang the Christ Child's shirts out to dry; and yet, just because tomorrow's Sunday and guests are coming, my hard-hearted mistress has told the cook that she wants to have me in tomorrow's soup, so I'm to have my head cut off this evening. So now I'm having a good crow while I still can.' 'Nonsense, Redcrest,' said the donkey, 'come along with us instead: we're going to Bremen, and any place'll suit you better than a stewpot. You've got a great voice, and when we all make music together, let me tell you, it'll certainly sound like something.' The cock thought this a sensible proposal, and all four of them went on their way together.

But they couldn't reach Bremen in one day, and in the evening they came to a forest and decided to spend the night there. The donkey and the dog lay down under a big tree, and the cat and the cock took to its branches, but the cock flew right to the top where he would be safest. Before going to sleep, he took one more look round in all directions and thought he saw a spark of light in the distance, so he called out to his companions that there must be a house not far away because he could see a light burning. The donkey said: 'Then we must get on our feet and go to it, because we've got a pretty poor lodging here.' The dog said he wouldn't mind either if he could have a bone or two, with some meat on them. So they set off in the direction of the light, and soon enough it was getting brighter, and it got bigger and bigger till they came to a well-lit house where a band of robbers lived. The donkey, being the tallest, went up to the window and looked in. 'What do you see, Greyskin?' asked the cock. 'What do I see?' exclaimed the donkey. 'I see a table laid with fine food and drink, and a pack of robbers sitting round it enjoying themselves.' 'That would be something for us,' said the cock. 'Yes, yes, my goodness, I wish we were there!' said the donkey. So the animals put their heads together to decide what would be the best way of driving the robbers out of the house, and at last they thought of a plan. The donkey had to stand with its front feet against the window, the dog had to jump onto the donkey's back and the cat climb onto the dog, and finally the cock flew up and perched on the cat's head. When they had done that, one of them gave a signal, and all together they began making their music: the donkey brayed, the dog barked, the cat mewed and the cock crowed, and then they all crashed into the room through the window, smashing the panes to smithereens. At this bloodcurdling din the robbers started to their feet, thinking some hobgoblin had broken into the house, and rushed out into the wood in a panic. Whereupon our four friends sat down at the table, made the best of what was left, and ate as if they had a month's fast ahead of them.

When our four minstrels had finished their meal, they put out the light and looked for sleeping quarters, each according to his natural needs and preferences. The donkey lay down on the dung-heap, the dog behind the door and the cat near the warm ashes on the hearth, while the cock went to its roost among the rafters; and being tired after their long journey, they soon fell asleep. When midnight was past and the robbers, watching from a safe distance, noticed that the house was now dark and that all seemed quiet, their captain said: 'Well now, we shouldn't have let ourselves be frightened off like that,' and he ordered one of his men to go back to the house and investigate. The man found the whole place lying silent, went into the kitchen to fetch a light, mistook the cat's fiery red eyes for live coals and tried to light a match at them. But the cat wasn't to be trifled with like this, and leapt at his face spitting and scratching. At this he panicked, took to his heels and tried to leave by the back door, but the dog was lying there and jumped up and bit him in the leg. He ran for his life across the yard, and just as he was passing the dung-heap he got a mighty kick in the backside from the donkey; meanwhile the cock, perching on its roost and wakened by the noise, began screeching: 'Kikiriki-kee! Kikiriki-kee!' The robber ran back as fast as he could to his captain and said: 'Oh my God, there's some horrible witch sitting in the house who hissed at me and scratched my face with her long nails, and there's a man with a knife standing by the door who stabbed me in the leg, and a black monster in the yard who started beating me with a wooden club, and up in the roof there's the judge sitting, and he called out: "Bring the thief to me! Bring the thief to me!" So I got away while the going was good.' After that the robbers didn't dare enter the house again, but the four members of the Bremen town band so much enjoyed living there that they just stayed on.

> And for many a year this tale has been told;
> The last tongue to tell it's not yet cold.

Snowwhite

Once upon a time, in the middle of winter when the snow-flakes were falling from the sky like feathers, a queen sat sewing at a window with a frame of black ebony. And as she sewed and looked up at the falling snow, she pricked her finger with her needle, and into the snow there fell three drops of blood. The red looked so beautiful against the white that she thought to herself: If only I had a child as white as snow, as red as blood and as black as the wood of this window frame! Soon after this she gave birth to a little daughter who was as white as snow, as red as blood and had hair as black as ebony, and for this reason was called 'little Snowwhite'. And when the child was born the queen died.

A year later the king took another wife. She was a beautiful woman, but proud and haughty, and could not bear that anyone else's beauty should excel her own. She possessed a magic mirror, and when she stood in front of it and looked at herself she would say:

> 'Mirror, mirror on the wall,
> Who is the fairest of us all?'

The mirror would answer:

> 'My lady queen is the fairest of all.'

And this satisfied her, for she knew that the mirror spoke the truth.

But Snowwhite was growing up and becoming more and more beautiful, and by the age of seven she was as lovely as the bright day and more beautiful even than the queen. One day when the queen asked her mirror:

> 'Mirror, mirror on the wall,
> Who is the fairest of us all?'

it answered:

> 'My lady queen is fair to see,
> But Snowwhite is fairer far than she.'

At this the queen took fright and turned yellow and green with envy. From now on, whenever she saw Snowwhite, her heart turned over inside her, she hated the girl so. And envy and pride took root like weeds in her heart and grew higher and higher, giving her no peace by day or night. So she sent for a huntsman and said: 'Take that child out into the forest, I'm sick of the sight of her. You are to kill her and bring me her lungs and liver as proof.' The huntsman obeyed and took Snowwhite with him, but when he had drawn his hunting-knife and was about to thrust it into her innocent heart she began to cry and said: 'Oh, dear huntsman, let me live; I will run away into the wild forest and never come home again.' And because she was so beautiful the huntsman took pity on her and said: 'Run away then, you poor child.' The wild beasts will soon have eaten you, he thought, and yet it was as if a stone had been rolled from his heart because he did not have to kill her. And when a young boar happened to come bounding up he slaughtered it, cut out its lungs and liver and took them to the queen as the proof she wanted. The cook was ordered to stew them in salt, and the wicked woman devoured them, thinking she had eaten the liver and lungs of Snowwhite.

And now the poor child was utterly alone in the huge forest, and so terrified that she gazed at every leaf on the trees, trying to think what to do to save herself. Then she began to run, and she ran over the sharp stones and through the thorns, and the wild animals bounded past her but did not harm her. She ran on as far as her feet would carry her, until it was nearly evening: then she saw a little cottage and went into it to rest. Inside the cottage everything was tiny, but more dainty and neat than you can imagine. There stood a little table with a white table-cloth and seven little plates, every plate with its little spoon, and seven little knives and forks and cups as well. In a row along the wall stood seven little beds all made up with sheets as white as snow. Because she was so hungry and thirsty, Snowwhite ate a little of the vegetables and bread from each plate and drank a sip of wine from each of the cups; for she didn't want to take the whole of anyone's supper. Then, because she was so tired, she lay down on one of the little beds – but none of them fitted her: one was too long, the next too short, till finally the seventh was the right size. So in it she stayed, and said her prayers and went to sleep.

When it had got quite dark, the owners of the little house came home: they were the seven dwarfs who worked in the hills, hacking and digging out precious metal. They lit their seven lamps, and as soon as there was light in the cottage they saw that someone had been there, because not everything was exactly as they had left it. The first said: 'Who's been sitting on my chair?' The second said: 'Who's been eating from my plate?' The third said: 'Who's taken some of my bread?' The fourth said: 'Who's eaten some of my vegetables?' The fifth said: 'Who's been poking with my fork?' The sixth said: 'Who's been cutting with my knife?' The seventh said: 'Who's been drinking out of my cup?' Then the first of them looked round and saw that there was a little hollow on his bed, and he said: 'Who's stepped on my bed?' The others came running up and exclaimed: 'Someone's been in mine too.' But when the seventh looked at his bed he saw Snowwhite lying there asleep. And he called the others, who came running up and cried out in amazement; they fetched their seven little lamps and shone them on Snowwhite. 'Oh goodness me! Oh goodness me!' they cried. 'What a lovely girl!' And they were so delighted that they didn't wake her, but let her go on sleeping in the little bed. But the seventh dwarf slept with his companions, one hour with each of them, and so the night passed.

When it was morning Snowwhite woke up, and when she saw the seven dwarfs she was scared. But they spoke to her kindly and asked her what her name was. 'I'm called Snowwhite,' she replied. 'How did you get into our house?' asked the dwarfs. So she told them how her stepmother had tried to have her killed, but that the huntsman had spared her life, and then she had wandered all day till finally she found their cottage. The dwarfs said: 'If you will keep house for us, and do the cooking and the beds and the washing and the sewing and the knitting, and keep everything neat and tidy, you can stay with us and you shan't want for anything.' 'Yes,' said Snowwhite, 'I'd like that very much.' So she stayed with them, and looked after their cottage. In the morning they went into the hills and dug for ore and gold, in the evening they came back and their supper had to be ready. The young girl was by herself all day, and the kind dwarfs warned her and said: 'Beware of your stepmother, she will soon find out that you are here; don't on any account let anyone in.'

But after the queen, as she supposed, had eaten Snowwhite's liver and lungs, her first thought was she was again the most beautiful of all women, and she stood before her mirror and said:

> 'Mirror, mirror on the wall,
> Who is the fairest of us all?'

And the mirror answered:

> 'My lady queen is fair to see:
> But Snowwhite lives beyond the hills,
> With the seven dwarfs she dwells,
> And fairer far than the queen is she.'

Then the queen took fright, for she knew that the mirror never told a lie, and she realized that the huntsman had deceived her and that Snowwhite was still alive. So she began plotting and planning again how to kill her; for so long as she was not the fairest of all, her envy never left her in peace. And having finally thought of a plan, she painted her face and disguised herself as an old pedlar-woman, and no one could have recognized her. In this disguise she went over the seven hills to the house of the seven dwarfs, knocked at the door and called out: 'Fine wares for sale, for sale!' Snowwhite peeped out of the window and called to her: 'Good day, old lady, what have you got to sell?' 'Fine wares, lovely things,' she answered, 'laces of all colours' – and she fetched out one that was made of many-coloured silk. I can let in this honest woman, thought Snowwhite, and she unbolted the door and bought the pretty lace. 'My child,' said the old woman, 'how untidy you look! Come, I'll lace you up properly.' Snowwhite suspected nothing, stood in front of the old woman and let herself be laced with the new lace; but the old woman laced her up very fast and pulled the lace so tight that Snowwhite's breath was stopped and she fell down as if dead. 'Now you're no longer the fairest of us all,' said the queen and hurried out.

Not long after, when evening fell, the seven dwarfs came home: but what a fright they got when they saw their dear little Snowwhite lying on the ground, not moving or stirring, as if she were dead! They lifted her up, and seeing that she was laced too tightly they cut the laces – then she began to breathe a little, and gradually she came back to life. When the dwarfs heard what had happened they said: 'That old pedlar-woman was the godless queen and no one else – be on your guard and let no one in here when we're not with you.'

But when the evil woman got home, she went to her mirror and asked:

> 'Mirror, mirror on the wall,
> Who is the fairest of us all?'

And the mirror answered as before:

> 'My lady queen is fair to see:
> But Snowwhite lives beyond the hills,
> With the seven dwarfs she dwells,
> And fairer far than the queen is she.'

When the queen heard that, she was so startled that all the blood rushed to her heart, for she saw very well that Snowwhite had come to life again. 'But now,' she said, 'I'll think out something that will deal with you once and for all.' And by the witchcraft she knew she made a poisoned comb. Then she disguised herself and took the form of another old woman. And again she went over the seven hills to the house of the seven dwarfs, knocked at the door and called out: 'Fine wares for sale, for sale!' Snowwhite peeped out and said: 'Go away, I'm not allowed to let anyone in.' 'Surely they'll allow you to take a look,' said the old woman, and pulled out the poisoned comb and held it up. The young girl liked it so much that she let herself be fooled and opened the door. When they had agreed on a price the old woman said: 'Now I'll comb your hair properly for you.' Poor Snowwhite suspected nothing and let the old woman have her way; but she had hardly stuck the comb into her hair when its poison worked and the young girl fell senseless to the ground. 'That's done for you now, my beauty queen,' said the wicked woman, and off she went. But fortunately it was nearly evening and the seven little dwarfs were coming home. When they saw Snowwhite lying on the floor as good as dead, they suspected her stepmother at once, and searched and found the poisoned comb, and as soon as they had pulled it out of her hair Snowwhite revived and told them what had happened. Then they warned her again to be on her guard and not to open the door to anyone.

Back home the queen stood before her mirror and said:

'Mirror, mirror on the wall,
Who is the fairest of us all?'

And it answered as before:

> 'My lady queen is fair to see:
> But Snowwhite lives beyond the hills,
> With the seven dwarfs she dwells,
> And fairer far than the queen is she.'

When she heard the mirror say this, she trembled and shook with fury. 'Snowwhite shall die,' she cried, 'even if it costs me my own life.' With that she went to a completely secret remote room which no one else ever entered, and there she made an apple filled with deadly poison. Outwardly it looked like a beautiful white-and-red-cheeked apple which made everyone who saw it want to take a bite out of it, but anyone who did so was doomed. When the apple was ready, she painted her face and disguised herself as a peasant woman, and then she went over the seven hills to the house of the seven dwarfs. When she knocked, Snowwhite put her head out of the window and said: 'I can't let anyone in, the seven dwarfs have told me I mustn't.' 'That's all right,' answered the peasant woman, 'I'll have no difficulty selling my apples. Here, I'll make you a present of one.' 'No,' said Snowwhite, 'I'm not allowed to take anything.' 'Are you afraid it's poisoned?' said the old woman. 'Look here, I'll cut the apple in two: you eat the red cheek and I'll eat the white one.' But the apple was so cunningly made that only the red cheek was poisoned. Snowwhite was longing to eat this lovely apple, and when she saw the peasant woman doing so she could resist no longer, put her hand out and took the poisoned half. But no sooner did she have a bite in her mouth than she fell to the floor dead. Then the queen gazed at her gloatingly and laughed a dreadful laugh and said: 'White as snow, red as blood, black as ebony! This time the dwarfs won't wake you.' And when she got home and asked the mirror:

> 'Mirror, mirror on the wall,
> Who is the fairest of us all?'

it at last answered:

> 'My lady queen is the fairest of all.'

And then her envious heart was at rest, if an envious heart ever can be.

When the dwarfs came home in the evening, they found Snowwhite lying on the ground, and not a breath stirring from her mouth, and she was dead. They lifted her up, looked all over her for something poisonous, unlaced her, combed her hair, washed her with water and wine, but it was all no good: the sweet girl was dead and dead she stayed. They laid her on a bier, and all seven sat by it and mourned her and wept for her for three days. Then they were going to bury her, but she still looked as fresh as a living person and still had her lovely red cheeks. They said: 'This is something we can't bury in the black earth,' and they had a transparent glass coffin made so that she could be seen from all sides; they laid her in it, and on it in letters of gold they wrote her name, and that she was a princess. Then they put the coffin out on the hill, and one of them always sat by it keeping watch. And the animals came too and mourned Snowwhite, first an owl, then a raven, and then a little dove.

So Snowwhite lay in her coffin for a long, long time; she didn't go bad, but just looked as if she were asleep, for she was still as white as snow, as red as blood and her hair was as black as ebony. Then it happened that a prince strayed into the forest and arrived at the dwarfs' house to spend the night there. He saw the coffin on the hill with the lovely Snowwhite inside, and read what was written on it in letters of gold. And he said to the dwarfs: 'Let me have that coffin, I'll pay you whatever you ask for it,' but the dwarfs answered: 'We wouldn't sell it for all the gold in the world.' So he said: 'Then give it to me, for I can't live without seeing Snowwhite, and I will honour her and treasure her as my dearest possession.' When he said that, the kind little dwarfs took pity on him and gave him the coffin. So the prince told his servants to carry it away on their shoulders. And it happened that they stumbled against a shrub and gave the coffin such a jolt that the lump of poisoned apple which Snowwhite had bitten off was jerked out of her throat. And presently she opened her eyes, pushed up the lid of the coffin and sat up and was alive again. 'Oh goodness, where am I?' she exclaimed. The prince's heart leapt with joy and he said: 'You are with me.' And he told her what had happened and said: 'I love you more than anything in the world: come with me to my father's palace, and you shall be my wife.' And Snowwhite liked him and went with him, and their wedding was prepared with great splendour and magnificence.

But Snowwhite's godless stepmother was asked to the feast too. So when she had put on beautiful clothes, she stood before the mirror and said:

'Mirror, mirror on the wall,
Who is the fairest of us all?'

And the mirror answered:

'My lady queen is fair to see:
But the young queen is fairer far than she.'

At this the evil woman shrieked out a curse and was beside herself with fear. At first she decided not to go to the wedding at all, but the thing preyed on her mind and she just had to go to see the young queen. And when she entered she recognized Snowwhite and stood rooted to the spot with fright and terror. But already a pair of iron slippers had been heated over glowing coals and they were brought in with tongs and placed before her. Then she had to put her feet into the red-hot shoes and dance till she dropped dead.

Lazy Harry

Harry was so lazy that although he had nothing else to do but drive his goat out to graze every day, he still heaved many a sigh when he got back home in the evening after completing his day's labours. 'What a weary job it is,' he would say, 'what a terrible burden, year after year, driving that goat out into the fields every day till Michaelmas! If I could even lie down and take a nap while she feeds! But no, I've got to keep my eyes open or she'll damage the young trees, or squeeze through a hedge into someone's garden, or even run away altogether. What sort of a life is that? No peace of mind, no relaxation.' He sat down and collected his thoughts and tried to work out some way of getting this burden off his back. For a long time all his ponderings were in vain, then suddenly the scales seemed to fall from his eyes. 'I know what I'll do!' he exclaimed. 'I'll marry Fat Katie; she's got a goat as well, so she can take mine out with hers and I won't have to go on wearing myself to a shadow like this.'

So Harry got up, set his weary limbs in motion and walked right across the street, for it was no further than

that to where Fat Katie's parents lived; and there he asked
for the hand of their hard-working, virtuous daughter.
Her parents didn't stop to think twice; 'Like to like makes
a good match,' they remarked, and gave their consent.
So now Fat Katie became Harry's wife and drove both
the goats out to graze. Harry spent his days very pleas-
antly, with nothing more strenuous to recover from than
his own idleness. He only went out with her now and
then, saying: 'I'm just doing this so that I'll enjoy my bit
of a rest afterwards all the more; you lose all your appre-
ciation of it otherwise.'

But Fat Katie was no less idle than Harry. 'Harry dear,'
she said one day, 'why should we needlessly make our
lives a misery like this and spoil the best years of our
youth? Those two goats wake us out of our best morning
sleep anyway with their bleating: wouldn't it be better to
give them both to our neighbour and get a beehive from
him in exchange? We'll put up the beehive in a sunny
place behind the house and just leave it to look after itself.
Bees don't need to be minded and taken out to graze:
they'll fly out and find their own way home and make
honey, without our having to raise a finger.' 'You're a very
sensible girl,' answered Harry, 'and we'll do as you sug-
gest right away. What's more, honey's tastier than goat's
milk and it does you more good and you can store it for
longer.'

The neighbour willingly gave them a beehive in
exchange for their two goats. The bees flew in and out

tirelessly from early in the morning till late in the evening and filled the hive with the finest honey, so that in the autumn Harry was able to collect a whole jar of it.

They stood the jar on a shelf that was fixed to the wall above their bed; and fearing that someone might steal it or the mice might get at it, Katie fetched in a sturdy hazel rod and put it at the bedside, so that she wouldn't have to bestir herself unnecessarily but just reach for it and drive away any unwelcome visitors without having to get up.

Lazy Harry didn't like to rise before midday: 'Too soon out of bed and you'll soon be dead,' he would remark. So there he was one morning, still lolling among the feathers in broad daylight, having a good rest after his long sleep, and he said to his wife: 'Women have a sweet tooth, and you've been at that honey again: I think our best plan, before it all gets eaten up by you, would be to give it in exchange for a goose and a young gander.' 'But not till we have a child to mind them!' replied Fat Katie. 'You don't suppose I'd want to be bothered with young goslings, needlessly wearing out my strength?' 'And do you suppose,' said Harry, 'that the boy will look after geese? Nowadays children don't do what they're told any more, they do just as they please, because they think they're cleverer than their parents, just like that farmhand who was sent to fetch a cow and started chasing three blackbirds.' 'Well then,' answered Katie, 'this one had better look out if he doesn't do as I tell him. I'll take a stick to him and give his hide a real good tanning. Watch me, Harry!' she exclaimed in her excitement, seizing the stick she kept to drive away the mice, 'watch me beat the backside off him!' She lifted the stick, but unfortunately struck the honey-jar above the bed. The jar was knocked against the wall and fell to smithereens, and all that fine honey went trickling over the floor. 'Well, so much for the goose and the young gander,' said Harry, 'we shan't have to mind them now. But it's a bit of luck that the jar didn't fall on my head; we've every cause to be content with our lot.' And seeing that some honey was still left in one of the fragments, he reached out and picked it up and said cheerfully: 'Wife, let's enjoy the little that's left over here, and then take a bit of a rest after the fright we've had. What does it matter if we get up a little later than usual, the day's still long enough.' 'Oh yes,' answered Katie, 'better late than never. You know the one about the snail that was invited to the wedding? It set out and got there in time for the christening. And just outside the house it fell from the top of a fence, and said to itself: "More haste, less speed."'